A Long Road
on a
Short Day

A Long Road on a Short Day

GARY D. SCHMIDT
& ELIZABETH STICKNEY

WITH ILLUSTRATIONS BY EUGENE YELCHIN

CLARION BOOKS | HOUGHTON MIFFLIN HARCOURT | BOSTON   NEW YORK

ONE

Early on a white January morning, Samuel's mother said, "I do wish we had a brown-eyed cow to give us milk for the baby."

Samuel's father set down his mug.

"And for your tea," she said.

Samuel's father smiled and got up from the table. He took his best Barlow knife from the mantel and said to Samuel, "Dress warm if you're coming with me."

Samuel ran to get his coat off the hook. "Where are we going, Papa?"

"To find that brown-eyed cow for your mother," Papa said.

Mama pulled Samuel's scarf into a warm knot and hugged him. "Take some apples with you," she said. "You'll be hungry."

Samuel and Papa each took two apples. Then they said goodbye to Mama and baby Ella and headed out into the cold.

The sky was dark with clouds, and the wind was blowing the high pines back and forth. They passed their barn, where Star stood warm under his blanket, chewing hay. They passed their ice house, already filled with clear ice for next summer. They passed their maple sugar hut, where next month they'd boil and boil the sap away for syrup.

"Keep up," said Samuel's father. He looked up at the gray clouds. "It's a long road on a short day."

Samuel looked up at the gray clouds too. Then he hurried after Papa.

TWO

The road led them to Frank Snow's place, where Hallie Girl, Mr. Snow's collie, was up on her toes, wagging her tail and yipping to let Mr. Snow know about their visitors. They followed her to the tie-up behind the Big Barn, where Mr. Snow was milking Daisy, a black-and-white heifer.

"They say a storm is on its way," Mr. Snow

said. "What business takes you from a warm fireside?"

"I'm looking to make a trade," Samuel's father said, eyeing Daisy. He took out his shiny Barlow knife.

Mr. Snow stood up from the milking stool. He took Papa's knife and opened it. He ran his finger along the sharp blade. "Jonathan," he said, "I'd have use for a knife good as this. Would you take two tin lanterns in exchange?"

"I'd like to see them," Papa said.

"They're hanging on the wall in the back shed," Mr. Snow said. "Samuel, would you bring them for your father to look at?"

Samuel and Hallie Girl found the lanterns just where Mr. Snow said they would be. He carried them back to the tie-up, stopping to throw three snowballs to Hallie Girl, who caught each one and ate it.

"What do you think, Samuel?" Papa asked. "Are these a good trade for a Barlow knife?"

Samuel took off his mittens and ran a finger along the sides of one of the lanterns. He opened and shut the little door and opened and shut it again. Then he did the same with the second lantern.

Samuel looked up at his father. "I think it would be a good trade."

Mr. Snow and Papa smiled and shook hands. Mr. Snow shook Samuel's hand too.

Hallie Girl yipped again—and when Samuel knelt down and let her lick his face, he wished, just a little bit, it wasn't a brown-eyed cow his mother was wanting.

THREE

It was a whole lot colder when Samuel and his father left Mr. Snow's tie-up, each carrying a tin lantern. The clouds weighed down the sky, and Samuel wondered if the blowing trees would bend over beneath all that gray.

"Is our trading done?" Samuel asked.

Papa looked up at the dark sky. "The storm

may hold off yet," he said. "We'll stop to see the Perrys."

The first flakes of snow began to fall.

Samuel put out his tongue and tried to catch them.

"Keep up," said Papa. "It's a long road . . ."

". . . on a short day," said Samuel.

They turned onto Stone Hill Road and up to the Perrys' house. In the dark of the barn, Mr. Perry was threshing beans with his son, Georgie. "Welcome, Jonathan," said Mr. Perry. "I haven't seen a soul come up this road for a week or more—and none with tin lanterns!" He leaned against his flail.

"From Frank Snow," said Papa. "Good as new."

Samuel held his lantern up for Mr. Perry to see.

"We have kittens in the farther stall," said Georgie.

Papa nodded, and Samuel ran to find them. They were all black as night and hard to see in the shadows, so Samuel and Georgie knelt down and Samuel held out his hand. But the kittens arched their backs and hissed and ran against the back of the stall—all the kittens except one, who had a little bit of white around his nose. He tottered toward Samuel and leaned his head against his fingers.

They didn't have long to play. Samuel's father called before he had even held the white-nosed kitten.

Papa was still standing with Mr. Perry by the threshed beans, but he wasn't holding the two tin lanterns. Those were hanging from a beam. A bright candle was shining in each one, and the barn wasn't so dark anymore.

They walked together to the Perrys' house, and in the kitchen, Mrs. Perry handed Samuel a warm sugar doughnut. "Next time you'll come for a longer visit, Jonathan," she said.

Papa nodded.

"We can play with the kittens," said Georgie. "Maybe by then, they'll be old enough to leave their mother and you can take one home."

Samuel nodded, and he thought about the kitten with the little bit of white around his nose and wished again, just a little bit, it wasn't a brown-eyed cow his mother was wanting.

Then Mr. Perry handed Samuel's father a large blue book. "I hope you enjoy poetry," he said to Samuel.

Papa put the book under his coat.

Samuel, who did not want to lie, stayed as quiet as the white-nosed kitten.

FOUR

Samuel and his father waved goodbye to the Perrys, and when they reached Stone Hill Road, Samuel asked, "Did you make a good trade for Mr. Snow's lanterns?"

"I did—if we find someone in town interested in a book of British and American poems." He took the book from under his coat. Even under the gray sky, the gilt-edged pages flashed with light.

"Will we keep the book if no one wants it?"

"Your mother would be a little pleased if we did," said Papa. "But she'd be a little disappointed too."

Samuel tried to match his father's pace as they headed into town. More than a few snowflakes fell onto Samuel's nose and eyelashes, and he brushed them off with his wool mittens until the mittens started to get wet.

It wasn't too long before they came to a tall brick house, the first one in town.

"The Widow Mitchell's?" said Samuel.

Papa and Samuel walked up her porch steps.

"If she speaks to you, Samuel, you know how to be polite."

Samuel nodded. He could be polite. Even if no one he knew had ever been in the Widow Mitchell's house. *No one.*

He wondered if Georgie Perry would even believe him.

The Widow Mitchell answered the door when Samuel's father knocked. Her white hair was drawn into a tight bun at the back of her head, so tight it made her eyes look angry. Her dress was black, and a high collar cramped right up to her chin. She carried a black walking stick.

"What's all this?" she asked.

"You might remember me, Mrs. Mitchell.

Jonathan Hallett. I repaired your fence last spring."

"I don't remember you at all," said the Widow Mitchell. She pointed her black walking stick at Samuel. "And who is this boy tramping snow onto my porch?"

Samuel thought he had forgotten how to breathe.

FIVE

"This is my son," said Papa.

The Widow Mitchell looked at Samuel.

"And does your son have a name?" she said.

"My name is Samuel, Mrs. Mitchell."

"Is it now?" she said. "My husband's name was Samuel."

"Yes, ma'am," said Samuel. "I'll sweep off the porch, if I may borrow a broom."

The Widow Mitchell looked up at the clouds. "No need," she said. "A great deal more will be coming down before long."

"We've stopped to see if you might be interested in a trade," said Papa.

The Widow wrapped her dark shawl around herself. "I rarely trade," she said.

"So I understand," said Papa. "But I remember your library, and I wondered if you might be interested in a collection of poetry." He brought the Perrys' book out from under his coat.

The Widow Mitchell looked at the book. "You had better come inside," she said. "You as well, Samuel."

Samuel followed his father down the hallway. He passed paintings and small tapestries hanging on the walls. He passed mantels with silver candlesticks. He passed floors with thick red carpets. Finally, in a brightly lit room, the Widow Mitchell sat in a rocking chair and took the book. She opened it and began to read. Papa and Samuel waited, their hats in their hands.

"This is a splendid collection," said the Widow at last, "and a splendid book."

"I'm pleased you think so," said Papa.

The Widow looked at Samuel. "Samuel, in the kitchen, on a table by the window, there is a blue-and-white pitcher. Bring it here."

Samuel found the kitchen, and the pitcher, and brought it back to the bright room. He brought it back very carefully.

"I purchased this pitcher last spring, but I find it is too heavy for me to use when it is full."

Papa took the pitcher from Samuel. He turned it over in his hands.

"Samuel," said the Widow, "since you've come with your father this morning, you may just as well offer an opinion. Would you see the pitcher as a fair trade for this book?"

Samuel knew his mother would be happy with the blue-and-white pitcher, and it would not be too heavy for her to lift—even if it were full of creamy milk.

"I think it would be a fair trade," he said.

Samuel's father nodded.

"That is that, then," said the Widow Mitchell.

SIX

The Widow Mitchell was right: when they left her house, a dusting of snow had already covered the porch.

"Are we going home now, Papa?" asked Samuel.

"I wonder if Mr. Lewis would trade for the pitcher," said Papa.

"We're going to trade until we get ourselves a brown-eyed milk cow, aren't we?"

Papa looked up at the clouds. It was already past noon and they had only four hours of daylight left. Maybe not even that. "We'll see what Mr. Lewis has to say," said Papa.

But they had only gone a little way when they heard the sound of bells behind them. Samuel turned and saw Dr. Fulton's sleigh, pulled by a black mare. At first, Samuel thought the mare must be tired, the sleigh came on so slowly. But soon he saw what was holding her back. A fleecy ewe trailed on a short rope behind the sleigh.

"Jonathan, Samuel," nodded Dr. Fulton. "You're brave folks, walking so far from your

place on a day such as this." He brushed away the snow that had collected on the brim of his felt hat.

"You're out too," said Papa.

"But I'm on my way home—home from seeing the newest of our town's citizens into the world. And I've got a sheep in payment from her happy parents, as you can see."

Papa took off his glove and ran his hand over the sheep's back. "This is a fine merino, with a fleece thick and heavy. You'll likely get a good price for it come spring."

"I hope to be rid of the beast before then," said Dr. Fulton. "You wouldn't be interested in taking it off my hands?"

Papa smiled. "Do we have anything to offer, Son?"

Samuel carefully handed the Widow Mitchell's pitcher to Dr. Fulton. Then he walked to the mare's head and stroked her neck. She closed her eyes and leaned down to him.

"I'd call this a good bargain," said Dr. Fulton. "Shall we shake hands?"

Samuel reached into his pocket and found one of the apples. He took off his mitten, spread his palm wide, and held the apple up for the mare. And while Papa untied the merino sheep from the back of the sleigh, and while the mare munched the apple, Samuel wished again, just a little bit, it wasn't a brown-eyed cow his mother was wanting.

SEVEN

Lewis's General Store was on the same street as the Widow Mitchell's house. Mr. Lewis was on the front porch, sweeping as quickly as he could to keep up with the falling snow.

"You'll be sweeping until dark if you hope to keep that porch clear," said Papa.

"You're right. But when the snow piles up,

customers stay away. So what brings you two into town?"

"We're hoping to trade," said Papa. "We wondered if you might be interested in this merino."

Mr. Lewis shook his head. "I don't trade in livestock," he said. "You'd be better off going to the farms around town."

"I thought of that," said Papa. "But as I recall, Mrs. Lewis is a fine weaver, and the wool from a merino sheep is soft and strong."

Mr. Lewis came down the steps. He took off his glove and ran his fingers over the sheep's back.

"I don't have the space to pasture it," he said.

"Sheep don't take much room. And you could find someone outside of town who'd be glad to keep her for you come spring. Samuel here would be a good one to tend it."

Mr. Lewis looked at Samuel. "What do you say, boy? Would you be willing to care for this sheep for me come spring?"

Samuel looked at the merino. He had cared for roosters and hens and geese. He had kept four snakes and five turtles. He had twice ridden the Chamberlains' plow horses. There wasn't a cat he wouldn't play with. And dogs? Dogs were the best living things God had ever made.

But sheep, he thought, smelled. And they were stupid.

"I'd be willing," Samuel said.

"Fine. You take the sheep around back while your father and I finish our business.

There's a pen in the old stable where you can put her. And a bale of hay to spread out." Then Mr. Lewis and Papa went into the store.

Samuel pulled on the rope. "Come on, sheep," he said. "Move."

The sheep did not move.

"It's warm in the stable," said Samuel, and he tugged a little harder.

The sheep did not move.

Samuel went around to the back end of the sheep and pushed.

The sheep startled forward, and Samuel fell face first into the snow.

Sheep were really stupid.

And they smelled.

EIGHT

When Samuel had penned the merino sheep and come out of the stable, Papa was smiling.

"Samuel, I know exactly where we should go next," he said, and he handed Samuel a wedge of dark cheese.

"You traded for cheese?" said Samuel.

"I hope I'm a better trader than that," said

Papa, and he pulled out a gold pocket watch.

Samuel wondered if a pocket watch might trade for a mare. Or maybe a sheepdog to help take care of the merino. Or at least a white-nosed kitten.

"I thought we'd go talk with Mr. Everett about one of his dairy cows," said Papa. "And if not Everett, perhaps Mr. Buxton beyond him."

Samuel's feet were cold and tired, and they dragged a little in the snow collecting on the road. "It's a long road, Papa," said Samuel.

"On a short day," said Papa.

The wind was up now, and Samuel knotted his scarf a little tighter around his neck. He and his father each ate a wedge of cheese and an apple.

"What if Mr. Everett doesn't want the watch?" said Samuel.

"That's possible," said Papa. "Farmers and dairymen don't cater to watches much. We know what time it is by the sun."

Samuel looked up into the sky. Even though the clouds were thick and dark, he knew it was probably close to two o'clock. Maybe a little later.

He wasn't sure that Mr. Everett would want a pocket watch.

When they came out of town, he still wasn't sure Mr. Everett would want a pocket watch.

When they crossed the Wire Bridge, he still wasn't sure Mr. Everett would want a pocket watch.

When they climbed Hurd Hill, he sure did hope that Mr. Everett would want a pocket watch after they had come all that way.

"Nearly there," said Papa. "If it wasn't snowing so hard, you'd be able to see the house."

And Papa was right: soon they were knocking on the Everetts' door, and Mrs. Everett was unfastening Samuel's jacket and unknotting his scarf and asking if he'd rather have his hot milk plain or with cocoa powder mixed in and saying that he'd done well to come so far with his father when the weather was this cold and wet.

Samuel decided he liked Mrs. Everett very much. "With cocoa powder," he said.

He surely, surely did hope that Mr. Everett would want a pocket watch.

NINE

Samuel was sipping his cup of cocoa—it was very hot—when he heard the word "pony."

"Not much use to us anymore," Mr. Everett said, "since Mariella grew up and got herself married. Mother drives the horses, same as me, when she needs to go to town. The cart hasn't been out in ages."

Samuel tried to sip his cocoa quietly. A cart!

"And the pony is a good little thing. She'd be gentle as can be with young Samuel."

A pony and a cart! It was all Samuel could do not to say it was a good trade and they'd take it.

But Samuel's father seemed to think it a good trade too. "I guess you've made us a fair offer. Do you agree, Samuel?"

Samuel nodded. He didn't trust himself to say anything at all.

He imagined that when spring came and he was finished taking care of the merino for the day, he could drive the pony and cart over to the Perrys' and play with the kittens. In summer, he could ride the pony around the fields, looking for blueberries. Maybe he could race

Dr. Fulton's mare—not that he'd win, but just to race!

"I think we have an agreement, then," Mr. Everett said. "This watch is just what I've been looking for."

Papa smiled. "Samuel, it's time to be on our way. The sun will be down before we're ready for it."

Samuel nodded. "It's a long road on a short day," he said. He gulped the last of his cocoa and thanked Mrs. Everett. She helped him into his winter things, handed Samuel the mittens she'd been drying over the wood stove, and knotted his scarf around him.

"Be careful out in the storm," she said.

By the time Samuel was ready, Mr. Everett

had brought the cart and pony into the yard. "Her name is Dolly," he told Samuel.

"Dolly is a good name for a pony," said Samuel.

Papa gave him the last apple, and Samuel fed it to Dolly. Then he got in the cart and took the reins, and Papa walked by Dolly's head.

TEN

When they came out onto the road, it was getting harder to see, since now the snow held steady and the sun was low. They looked up the hill toward Mr. Buxton's dairy farm and down the road toward home.

Papa stopped and turned to Samuel. "Son, we have a decision to make. I'd like to keep this pony and cart, but they're not what your mother wanted."

Samuel looked at Dolly. He looked at the reins in his hands. "I could be more help around the farm with this pony and cart," he said.

"That's so," said Papa.

"And I don't suppose we'll ever have a chance like this again," said Samuel.

"That's so as well. At least, not until you'd be tall enough to ride a full-size horse."

"But that won't be very long from now, will it?"

Papa smiled. "Not very long at all. And no one could dispute the fact that you've done a man's job today."

"Do you think Mr. Buxton would trade us a milk cow for Dolly and her cart?"

"We won't know until we ask," Papa said.

The road led up the hill and past a forest of tall white pines. The branches dipped under the snow that fell thick upon them, and sometimes they sprang up when a gust blew the flakes off into a whirlwind.

Dolly walked steadily on the slick road. Samuel felt her sureness through the reins, even when she tossed her head back and forth to shed the snow. She was a good pony, and Samuel wished again, just a little bit, it wasn't a brown-eyed cow his mother was wanting.

ELEVEN

Mr. Buxton was in his barn, beginning evening chores. "Good to see you," he called. "A welcome surprise. Stay for supper. Two more would be no trouble at all."

Samuel's hands had gotten cold on the ride over, even though Mrs. Everett had dried his mittens. He half hoped Papa would say yes.

"Thank you," said Papa. "We need to be on

our way. But we're in hopes of a trade. We've found ourselves with a pony and cart."

"Jim Everett's?" Mr. Buxton said. "I've been meaning to ask him about that cart. My Peggy is almost old enough to drive it. It would be a help if she could get herself to school in the morning."

"Yes," said Papa. "The pony seems even-tempered."

Mr. Buxton jabbed his pitchfork into a haystack. "I wonder if you might be interested in trading for one of the young calves," he said. "Your boy could fatten it up for a year. She'd bring a good price at market."

Samuel thought of taking care of a merino sheep *and* a young calf on top of all his other chores.

"That would be a good trade," Papa said, "and Samuel would be a good hand at it. But we were in hopes of going home with a milk cow."

"That right, Samuel?" said Mr. Buxton.

"Yes, sir," said Samuel.

"You're not wanting that pony?"

Samuel looked at his papa, then at Mr. Buxton. "I do want the pony, but we need a milk cow."

"You have a baby sister at home, don't you?"

Samuel nodded.

"Jonathan," Mr. Buxton said, "it's a joy to any man to see his child grow like your young Samuel. He's taken a man's part, and you should be proud of him."

Papa nodded. Samuel knew he was.

"I believe I could part with one of my milk-ers," said Mr. Buxton, "seeing that Peggy would dearly love this pony and cart. Come to the tie-up and choose one that pleases you."

Samuel got off the cart. He wiped the snow off Dolly's back and he kissed her once, on the nose. Then he followed Papa into the barn.

They looked at two long rows of cows, all mooing for their supper. "What do you think, Samuel?" Papa said. "Which one do you like best?"

"And Samuel," said Mr. Buxton, "when you're done, I've got something else for you to choose."

TWELVE

The snow was falling fast and the light was almost gone when Samuel and his father turned toward home. They walked down Hurd Hill, past the tall white pines, past the Everetts' farm, toward the Wire Bridge and town. "Come, Bossy," said Papa.

"Come, Ned," said Samuel.

Bossy was the cow with the biggest and brownest eyes Samuel had ever seen.

And Ned was the border collie pup with the whitest collar around his shoulders and the whitest tip on his tail and the perkiest ears and the brightest eyes and the darkest coat Samuel had ever seen.

"We've had two litters this year," Mr. Buxton had said. "It would be a kindness if you would take one of these pups off my hands, young Samuel."

Samuel had hardly been able to speak. He had knelt down, and one of the pups—the one with the whitest collar and the whitest tip on his tail and the perkiest ears and the darkest coat—had bumbled up to him and licked his face.

Now Samuel and his father and Bossy and Ned walked over the Wire Bridge, and the wind pushed to get under Samuel's scarf.

"Bossy is hardly a proper name for a cow," said Samuel.

"Why don't you name her, then?" said his father. "You'll be the one doing the milking."

The snow swirled into Samuel's eyes.

"Blizzard," he said. "Let's call her Blizzard."

"A fine and proper name," said Samuel's father.

Back in town, the roads had already been rolled, so the walking was easier. They walked past Mr. Lewis's store, where all the lights were out. "I guess he figures there won't be anyone else out on this night," said Papa. They walked past the Widow Mitchell's house, and they saw her sitting near the lamp in the front window, reading.

Samuel and his father and Blizzard and Ned kept on toward home.

Out of town, the snow was deep again. They walked past the Perrys' place, and Samuel hoped the kittens would stay warm—especially the kitten with the little bit of white around his nose. Then they walked past the Snows' farm, and Hallie Girl came out to yip at them and wag her tail and nuzzle Ned.

Samuel and his father and Blizzard and Ned kept on toward home.

"I think I see the lights of our farm up ahead," said Samuel.

"And just in time," said his father. "This cold is more than enough for two men to bear."

They started to walk a little faster through the gathering snow. Ned ran on ahead, then came back to bark at them, then ran ahead, then came back to bark at them, until they were at their own farm, where every window in the house had a light glowing. And there was Mama opening the door to look out for them, and Ned bumbling up to her through the snow, and Blizzard mooing when she saw her new barn, and Mama with her hands up to her face. "Oh my!" she said. "Oh my!"

Samuel and Ned took Blizzard into her stall, and they spread hay for her, and Samuel pulled out one of Star's warm blankets for Ned to nestle into, and when he came back out of the barn, his father and his mother were still standing by the door, waiting for him.

"It's been a long road on a short day," said Samuel.

"Come inside and tell me all about it," said his mother.

And that is just what Samuel did.

For Dinah Stevenson,
editor extraordinaire
and friend
—G.D.S.

To Ezra —E.Y.

Clarion Books • 3 Park Avenue, New York, New York 10016
Text copyright © 2020 by Gary D. Schmidt • Illustrations copyright © 2020 by Eugene Yelchin

Clarion Books is an imprint of Houghton Mifflin Harcourt Publishing Company.

hmhbooks.com

The illustrations in this book were done in colored pencils, watercolor, gouache and were digitally assembled.
The text was set in Nimrod MT Std. • Book design by Sharismar Rodriguez

Library of Congress Cataloging-in-Publication Data
Names: Schmidt, Gary D., author. | Stickney, Elizabeth, author. | Yelchin, Eugene, illustrator.
Title: A long road on a short day / Gary D. Schmidt and Elizabeth Stickney; illustrated by Eugene Yelchin.
Description: Boston ; New York : Clarion Books, [2020] | Audience: Ages 7 to 9. | Audience: Grades 2–3.
Summary: On a short winter day, Samuel and his father enter into a series of trades with neighbors and strangers
until they come home with a brown-eyed milk cow for Mama. • Identifiers: LCCN 2019039826 (print) | LCCN
2019039827 (ebook) • ISBN 9780544888364 (hardcover) | ISBN 9780358378570 (ebook)
Subjects: CYAC: Barter—Fiction. | Fathers and sons—Fiction. Determination (Personality trait)—Fiction.
Country life—Fiction. Winter—Fiction. • Classification: LCC PZ7.S3527 Lo 2020 (print) | LCC PZ7.S3527 (ebook)
DDC [Fic]—dc23
LC record available at https://lccn.loc.gov/2019039826
LC ebook record available at https://lccn.loc.gov/2019039827

Manufactured in China
SCP 10 9 8 7 6 5 4 3 2 1
4500800797